Lynn Joseph

An Island Christmas

Illustrated by Catherine Stock

C L A R I O N   B O O K S

New York

To Ed and Jared,
forever and ever.

–L. Pokey/Mommy J.–

To Edouard, Francoise and Romaine, Peter and Judy,
Nanik, Daria, Mum, Wayne, Isa and Roland, Jude, Basil,
Bob and Victoria and the summer of '91.

–C.S.–

Clarion Books
a Houghton Mifflin Company imprint
215 Park Avenue South, New York, NY 10003
Text copyright © 1992 by Lynn Joseph
Illustrations copyright © 1992 by Catherine Stock

Printed in the USA.

Library of Congress Cataloging-in-Publication Data

Joseph, Lynn.
    An island Christmas / by Lynn Joseph ; illustrated by
Catherine Stock.
        p.   cm.
    Summary: Rosie's preparations for Christmas on the
island of Trinidad include picking red petals for the sorrel
drink, mixing up the black currant cake, and singing along
with the parang band.
    ISBN 0-395-58761-1
    [1. Trinidad and Tobago—Fiction.   2. Christmas—
Fiction.]   I. Stock, Catherine, ill.   II. Title.
PZ7.J77935Is   1992
[E]—dc20   91-16178
                                                        CIP
                                                         AC

W OZ   10 9 8 7 6 5 4 3 2 1

De first day of Christmas holidays
and de sun shining bright bright.
De sky blue for so.
"Is beach time!" I yell.
But Mama says, "No.
Plenty things to do, Rosie."
And she tie her apron strings tight.

"What kind of things?" I ask.
And Mama says with a smile,
"Well, we have to make de sorrel.
To drink with de Christmas pies."

3

"Sorrel, sorrel, red and sweet.
Sorrel, sorrel, melt de heat,"
I sing as I pick de sorrel fruit
off de plump, old sorrel tree.

Sugar Cane Man comes walking by
swinging his sugarcane bag.
"Ten cents a cane," he shouts,
waving a sugarcane high.

"Look at my sorrel, Mr. Sugar Cane Man."
I point to my bucket of fruit.
Sugar Cane Man give one big smile
and drop his burly brown bag.
He help me peel de red sorrel petals
off de fuzzy green seeds.

"Red, red, everything's red.
Fingers, toes, shirts and heads,"
I sing as de sorrel juice stains settle in.

Afterwards, Sugar Cane Man and me sit on de steps
sucking on two sweet sugarcanes.
We poke our canes in de pail of water
that drawing de juice
out of de red sorrel petals.

"Leave de sorrel. Let it draw in peace," says Mama.
She take de pail and set it on de kitchen counter.
"We'll bottle it tomorrow."

When Sugar Cane Man leaving,
he give Mama de biggest sugarcane in his bag.
"Merry Christmas," he says.
And Mama smile a sugar-wide smile.

De second day of Christmas holidays,
and Tantie come over early early.
"Like she 'fraid de sun go catch her,"
my brother Ragboy says.
"Is for de black currant cake," I whisper.
And I run down de stairs.

Mama, Tantie, and me take hold
of de heavy currant jar.
We empty de shiny black fruit into bowls.
De currants look like Christmas stars.
They been soaking since July
and now their juices running deep.
They mixing with de sorrel spice,
got de kitchen smelling sweet.

"Currants, currants, sticky and sweet.
Currants, currants, clump to my feet,"
I sing as Tantie stirs eggs and molasses
into de fruit bowls.
Mama bottles de sorrel
and I push in de bottle corks hard.
Then I line de cake pans with wax paper
and watch as Tantie swishes her mighty spoon
round and round each bowl.

Finally, Tantie pats down de last currant crumb.
De cakes sitting round and fat in their pans,
ready for de oven.
It's dark outside now, but de kitchen glowing
like Christmas.

Then we hear music.
"It's de parang band!" Daddy shouts.

De parang men coming!
They down in de streets
moving house to house
with de parang band beat.

De guitar men leading
with snip-snapping sounds.
De chou-chou men adding
their shake-shaking pounds.

Their shirts all colors
like flags in de night
weaving up de hill
till they stop at our light.

They stand round de gate
playing sweet Christmas tunes.
Me and Ragboy join in
with a glass and two spoons.

Mama clap her hands
and Daddy snap his fingers.
And Tantie sing de words
of de old Spanish traditions.

When de parang men finish playing
we hand them
fat ham and mustard sandwiches.
They eat, then move on,
their guitars singing "Merry Christmas!"
in de night air.

De next thing we know,
Christmas Eve gliding in
like a limbo dancer under de stick.

Mama hurry back and forth
making de alloe pies.
Me and Ragboy help—mashing potatoes and peppers.
Then Mama stuff them into pockets of dough,
and fry them up brown and crisp.

"Alloe pies, alloe pies, spicy and strong.
Eat with de sorrel so I don't burn my tongue,"
I sing as me and Ragboy crank de ice-cream maker.

Daddy forget a Christmas present,
so he gone off to town.
And still de Christmas tree to paint
before de sun go down.

"O Christmas tree, O Christmas tree,"
Ragboy sings as we drag out
de old guava branch
from inside de garage.
We stand it in a pot of dirt.
Ragboy hand me de white shoe polish
and I start painting de tree clean.

I paint over where Ragboy
spilled sorrel on a branch last year.
I paint over scratches
from de Christmas decorations.
And I paint over de notches we mark
for all de times de guava branch
been our Christmas tree.
Four notches so far.
Ragboy cuts one more notch
with a sharp bamboo stick.

Then we open Mama's Christmas bag.
It full up with shiny foil angels,
and round painted balls,
glittering marbles in net bags,
and coconut-shell dolls.
We hang them all up, then
throw small pieces of paper
high up in de air.
Our Christmas tree look covered with snow.

Afterwards, me and Ragboy run
to our mango tree house
to finish our Christmas presents.

I paint birds
on de shell earrings for Mama.
Ragboy add more tail
to de kite for Daddy.
Then we tie a big red bow round
de bucket of flowers we been growing since August.
Red hibiscus and golden buttercups,
white periwinkles and pink oleanders.
It's a Christmas bouquet for Tantie.

Finally, everything almost ready for Christmas!
Daddy come back from town
and wrap his secret present.
Mama bring out de alloe pies
and pour us each some sorrel.
And me and Ragboy hang de star
high on top de guava branch.
"O Christmas tree, O Christmas tree,"
Ragboy starts singing again.
This time, Mama, Daddy, and I join in.

Afterwards Mama clap her hands.
"Santa not coming to see
no wide-awake children," she say.
So me and Ragboy hurry
and get our good-night kisses.
Then we gone off to bed.
But we can't sleep,
so we stick de pillows over our heads
and whisper in de dark instead.

When Ragboy falls asleep
I think about de glorious black cake
waiting on de kitchen counter,
and de soursop ice cream cooling in de freezer.
Tomorrow taking too long to come.

De next thing I know
Ragboy tugging my hair.
"Wake up, Rosie. It's Christmas!"
he shout in my ear.

"Merry Christmas, Mama.
Merry Christmas, Daddy.
Merry Christmas, Ragboy.
Merry Christmas, Me!"
I sing as I chase Ragboy down de stairs.

And there in de living room
our tree glow so bright
from de sun shining in
fill up de branches with light.

"Look at all de presents
piled under de tree!" shouts Ragboy.
He finds a fire truck for him.
And Daddy's late present is
a steel drum for me.

Now I can make my own music!
And I wake de house playing
pom de dum dum pom pom
on my steel drum.

Mama and Daddy finally get up.
We pile them with presents and kisses and hugs.
Then Tantie come over,
aunts and uncles come next,
leading long lines of cousins
in their Christmas church best.
We hurry and get ready,
leave de house in a mess.
De shiny red paper and bows of all colors
lie scattered and rolling and falling all over.

In church we sing
Happy Birthday to Jesus
and listen to how
he was born in a manger.

After church we walk home
all hand in hand,
de sun shining down
on our Christmas island.

GLAMORGAN
POSTAL AGENCY
TIME OF CLEARANCE
M-F 115 PRES

30

A Note

Trinidad and Tobago are islands in the southern Caribbean Sea, off the coast of Venezuela. Together they make up a single republic. On these tropical islands, the temperature never dips below 75°F. Fruit trees and flowering shrubs cover the landscape with a cascade of colors. But there are no cold-weather trees, like firs and pines, on the islands. In Trinidad and Tobago, where it is summer all year round, the islanders use native plants—a large branch from a guava tree, or a small orange tree in a pot—as Christmas trees.

Among the most joyous holiday customs in the islands is one that originated with the early Spanish settlers—the parang bands. From the beginning of December until January 6, bands of people sing and play guitars, tambourines, and chou-chous, or maracas, in the streets and in concerts all over the islands. Some parang songs are sung in Spanish. Others have a Spanish rhythm or beat. Each year the bands perform brand-new songs along with the old favorites. The songs may be about any seasonal subject, such as the pork traditionally cooked for Christmas dinner, or Santa Claus. Nearly every song has an upbeat, foot-tapping tune that gets the people singing and dancing.

Christmas in Trinidad and Tobago wouldn't be the same without the wonderful foods that belong to the season. Black currant cake is a long-standing Christmas specialty prepared in almost every island home. The cakes are given as presents or served to visitors. And of course, a big one is always kept for the family to eat!

Sorrel, a special Christmas drink, is made from the red sepals of the sorrel plant. The mature sepals are peeled away from the seedpods and soaked in water for a few days to make a dark red, aromatic drink with a tangy taste. Sorrel is an annual plant, and the sepals are usually ready for picking around Christmastime.

Sugarcane and soursop ice cream are sweet treats eaten anytime, not only at Christmas. A great deal of sugarcane is grown in Trinidad. Most of it is processed to extract the sugar, which is then exported to other countries. But some is sold locally, and a person can cut a sugarcane stem, bite it, and suck the sweet juice from the "sticks"—fibers that resemble broomstraws—inside the cane. Soursop, a native tropical fruit, is dark green, oval-shaped, and about the size of a cantaloupe. It has a spiny surface, and the inside is white and thick like custard. It makes sweet, flavorful ice creams and shakes.

Jeffersonville Township
PUBLIC LIBRARY
jefflibrary.org